PULLEY

THIS BOOK BELONGS TO

_____

FOR MOM,

I think Mip and Pip would get along well with your fairies
and pea people. Thanks for all the inspiration
on our walks in the woods.

Running Press Kids
Hachette Book Group
1290 Avenue of the Americas, New York, NY 10104
www.runningpress.com/rpkids
@RP_Kids

Printed in China
First Edition: April 2019

Published by Running Press Kids, an imprint of Perseus Books, LLC,
a subsidiary of Hachette Book Group, Inc. The Running Press Kids name and logo
is a trademark of the Hachette Book Group.

The Hachette Speakers Bureau provides a wide range of authors for speaking events.
To find out more, go to www.hachettespeakersbureau.com or call (866) 376-6591.

The publisher is not responsible for websites (or their content)
that are not owned by the publisher.

Print book cover and interior design by Frances J. Soo Ping Chow.

Library of Congress Control Number: 2018935977

ISBNs: 978-0-7624-6299-5 (hardcover), 978-0-7624-6300-8 (ebook),
978-0-7624-6628-3 (ebook), 978-0-7624-6627-6 (ebook)

1010

10 9 8 7 6 5 4 3 2 1

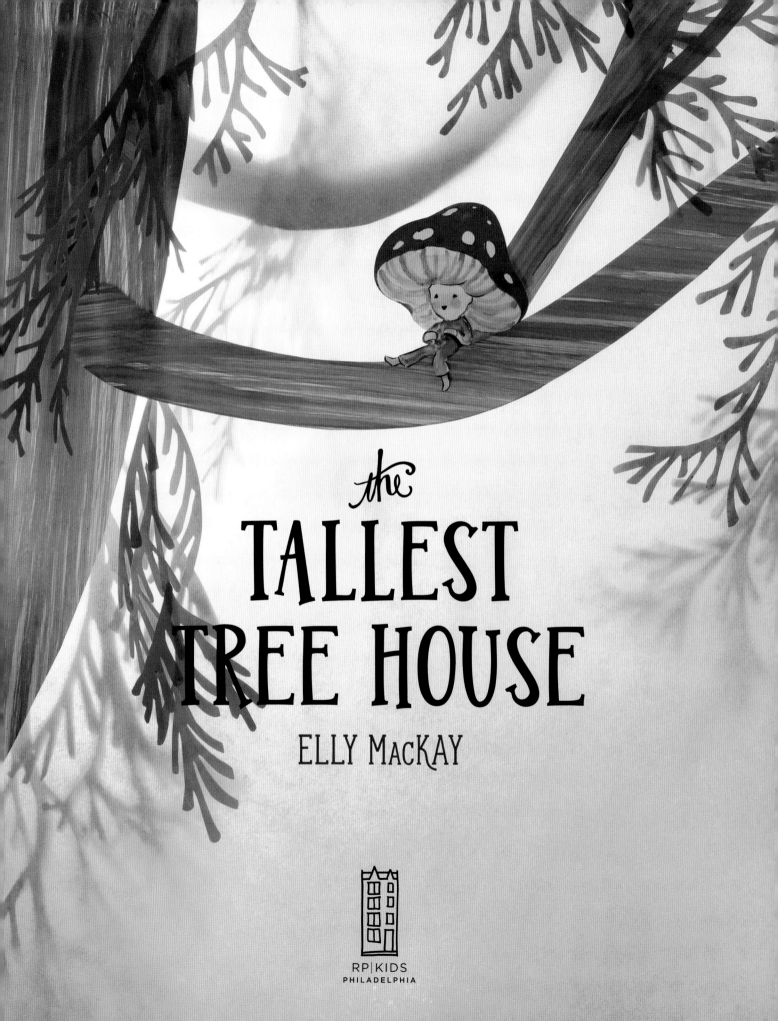

the TALLEST TREE HOUSE

ELLY MacKAY

RP|KIDS

PHILADELPHIA

Fairies are sometimes easy to miss.
But Mip was not one of them.

La La La
She could be heard singing above
the sound of the waterfall.

One day, she was flying around Inglis Falls,
looking for something to do when she spotted her best friend Pip.

"Hey, Pip! What are you reading?"

"It's a book on architecture."

"Buildings? I love to build things! Pip! We could build tree houses!"

cor · nice

cu · pola

can · ti · lever

"Building a tree house requires a great deal
of planning and hard work, Mip."

"Pip, I'm going to make the tallest tree house ever! I challenge you to a tree house race! Whoever makes the best tree house by sundown wins!"

The twigs of trees snapped. Mip sawed and hacked.
She carried and thwacked!

But Pip just sat on his rock and thought.
Then, he drew and measured and thought some more.

Mip zoomed around. Her tree house
was already taking shape.
She stopped for a moment to admire
her work. That is when she noticed
Pip was still sitting on the rock.

"Why haven't you started? You'll never win this way!"

"I'm planning. See, these are my blueprints, and they are almost ready.
Then, I can start building."

Mip glanced at Pip's drawings and then at her own tree house.
"I'm going to make mine even taller!"

While Mip zipped around, adding boards here and there,
Pip found a sturdy sapling

and began to build.

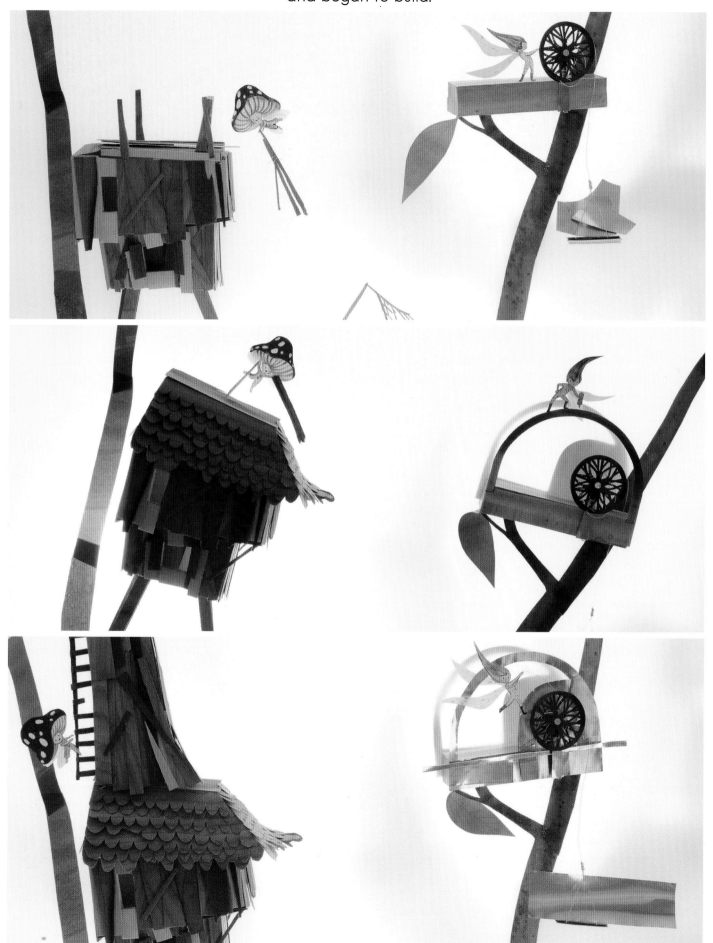

"With this tower, I'll win for sure!"

Gusts of wind sent sprays of mist over the rocks.
The leaves began to dance.

Pip leaned into the wind. He looked at Mip's tower
and began to worry.

"Mip, in this wind, I think you should tie down your tower."

"No, it would take too long. You're just trying to slow me down
so you have a chance at winning."

Even though it began to rain, Mip kept hammering, determined to win.

The wind roared and the tower
began to tremble, creak,
and sway.

Then the worst happened.
"Pip!"

The tower came crashing down!

Mip zoomed left and right, up and down, searching for Pip.
"Pip, are you all right?"

"Mip! Help! My wing is stuck."

Mip tied a rope around Pip's leg and, with lightning speed, she freed her friend.

"Thanks for working so fast to save me, Mip!"

"Pip, I'm so glad you are okay! I should have listened to you.
You were right about the tower."

They waited for the wind to settle down and
the rain to end. That is when Mip noticed something.
Not all was lost.

"The tower looks like a bridge. It connects our tree houses!
What if we worked together to make one tree house to share?"

With Mip's vision and imagination and Pip's careful planning
they came up with a new set of blueprints in no time.

Together, they worked tirelessly until sundown.
And when the tree house was finished, it was spectacular—

a winning piece of architecture.

"Pip, we are the best team ever!"
"Mip, that is exactly what I was thinking."

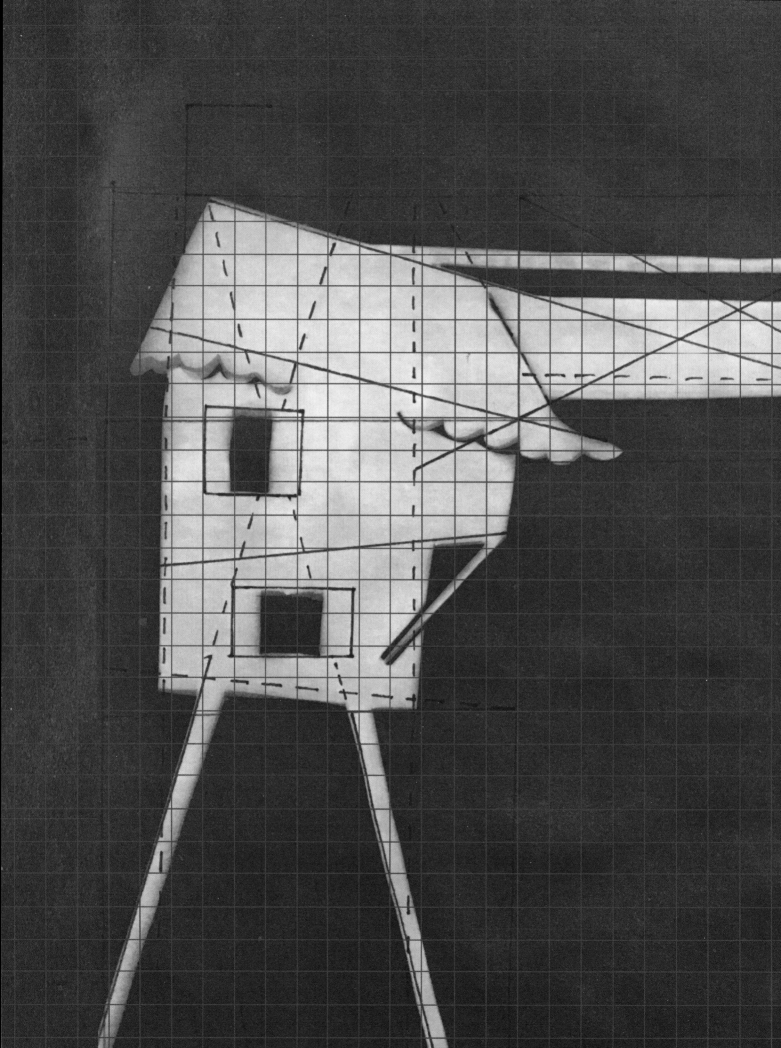

"Pip, we are the best team ever!"
"Mip, that is exactly what I was thinking."

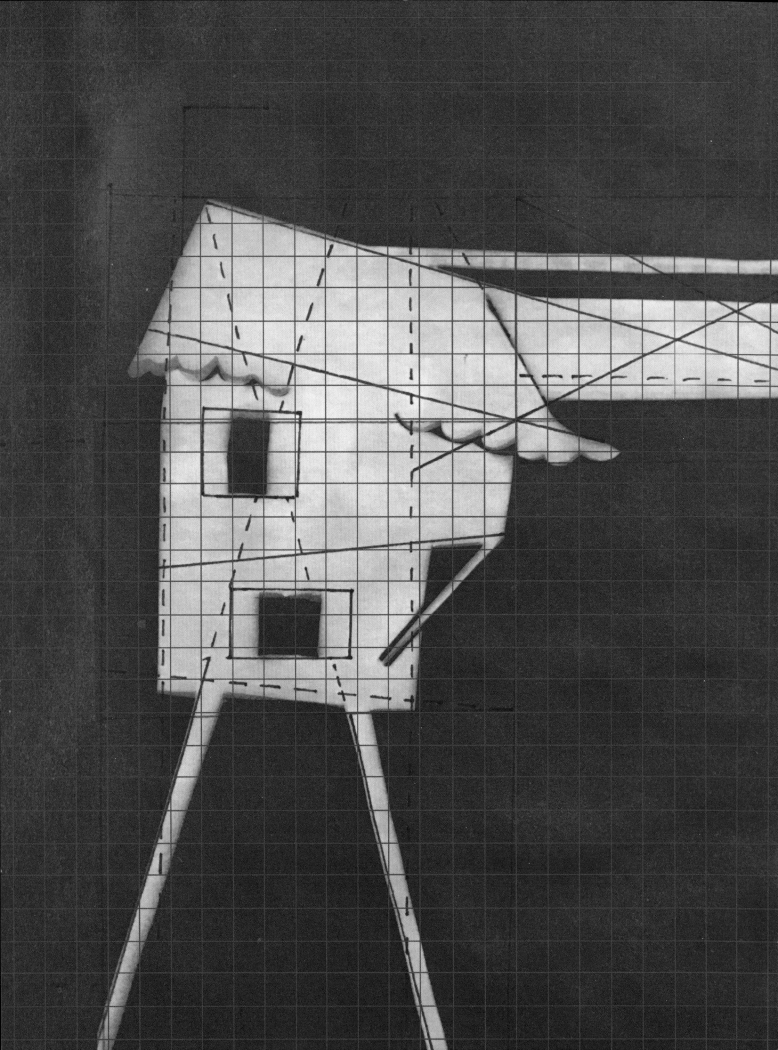